WAR AT THE ICE CREAM STORE 2

Rocky Road vs The Sundae Storm

By Cheryl DaVeiga
Illustrated by Nate Fakes

WAR AT THE ICE CREAM STORE RECAP

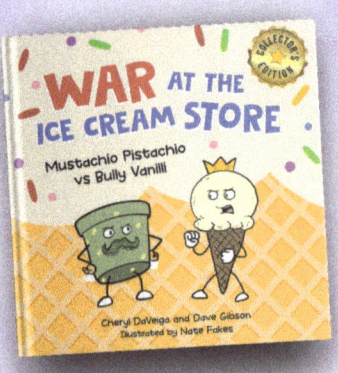

If you've already read and loved War at the Ice Cream Store, you will be delighted with this declicious sequel. Here's where we left off...

In an ice cream store called the Frozen Frogg, the ice cream king, Bully Vanilli, once ruled the frozen flavors.

But he was mean to his ice cream neighbors, especially the loneliest and least popular flavor, Mustachio Pistachio.

The courageous flavors and toppings revolted and stood up to Bully's bullying. Did Bully learn his lesson?

Well, he's now known as Vanilli Nice, and there has been peace in the freezer...

UNTIL...Wait! This is a nutty churn of events. The Frozen Frogg is hitting the news again. Let's go to the story...

MAJOR STORM ALERT!
BREAKING NEWS

Today may be the first sunny summer Sunday without ice cream—EVER!

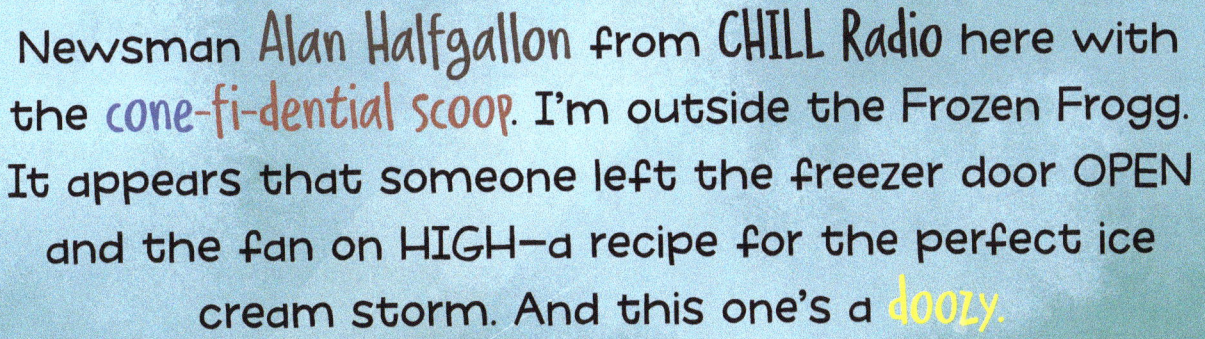

Newsman Alan Halfgallon from CHILL Radio here with the cone-fi-dential scoop. I'm outside the Frozen Frogg. It appears that someone left the freezer door OPEN and the fan on HIGH—a recipe for the perfect ice cream storm. And this one's a doozy.

Hurricane Doubledip is gaining strength and is headed from the open freezer door into the ice cream case.

It's *raining* buckets in there!

Cream is **whipping**.

Milk is **shaking**.

Cones are **breaking**.

The soft serve is **swirling** into a twister.

This could turn into a **legendairy superstorm!**

Here are the facts as we know them so far:

Vanilli Nice (formerly Bully Vanilli) was awakened early this morning by a banana-splitting…

He called 911.

Let's play the *tape*...

"Yikes! It's a perfect July ice cream day. Closing the Frozen Frogg would be a CATEGORY 5 DISASTER."

I'll send Sheriff Malt

and Deputy Doo-Dah

pronto—

and the

Sugar Clones and Storm Scoopers

just in case.

The line to get into the Frozen Frogg is **winding around** the block.

It's mayhem.

SCREECH

Wow, that whistle is loud. **Sheriff Malt** just arrived.

"Out of the way, Halfgallon!"
Sheriff Malt barks.

"Coming through..."

"Doo-Dah! —use your popsicle stick to pick that lock."

PICK, PICK! CLICK, CLICK!

"It's jammed," Deputy Doo-Dah sighs.

"Sugar Clones, stop waffling and break the door down!" orders Malt.

1 2 3

PUSH, PUSH!

BANG, BANG!

Not even a fudge of a budge.

"HELP!" cry the flavors and toppings.

"We're getting creamed in here!"

"Don't any of you ice creams have a lick of sense?" shouts Sheriff Malt. "Close the freezer door! And turn off that fan!"

"Any ideas from the flavors or toppings?" asks Mustachio Pistachio.

"We've got nothing."

"**Wait!**" cries Non-Dairy Strawberry.

"Don't we have a **heavyweight 10-gallon** fighting ice cream in the upstairs storage freezer?"

"Yes! Rocky Road!" they all squeal.

Non-Dairy Strawberry pulls the **red licorice laces** from her chunky shoes and tosses them to Rocky.

Rocky flings the laces in the air and lassoes the fan.

Rocky is on the ropes, bobbing and weaving in and out of the *spinning fan* blades.

The licorice is about to **SNAP!** Rocky leaps in the air, grabs the fan chain, and pulls it to the **OFF** position.

The gummies stick together below to make a fluffy landing pad. Rocky jumps.

PLOP!

"Ouch! That's a big boy!"

Rocky barrels over to the freezer door and gives it a **knockout** punch with all his heavyweight might.

BANG!

The door thumps shut.

A few final *flurries* fall.
A calm comes over the store. **Ahhhh...**
The flavors and toppings crawl back
into their glass showcase, and the
scoopers scoop up the mess.

"Yo, I did it,"
boasts Rocky...

"With a little help from my friends."
Vanilli Nice jiggles the lock
and yanks the front door open.
"The storm is over!" he announces.

So, in the end, everything's cool at The Frozen Frogg.
This is **Alan Half Gallon** chillin' out.

WAR AT THE ICE CREAM STORE

Mustachio Pistachio vs Bully Vanilli

Collector's Edition

reillustrated with enhanced story + bonus content!

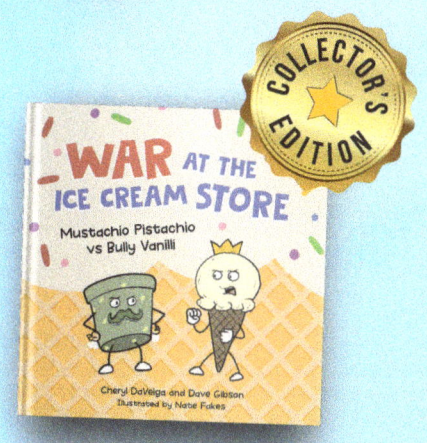

Jump on over to BiffBamBooza.com for more titles, sing-along songs, and giggles.

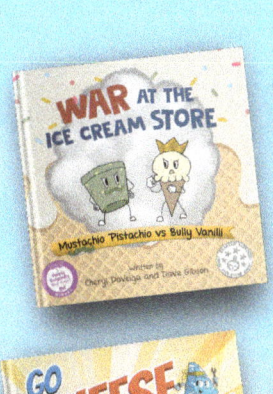
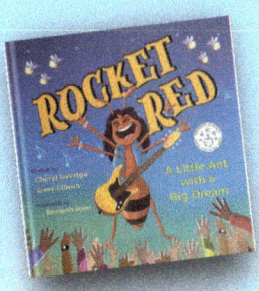

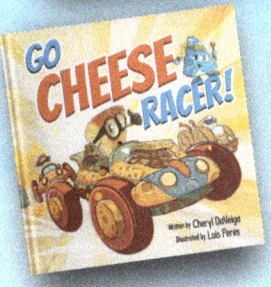

About the Author

Cheryl DaVeiga is an award-winning songwriter and children's book author who loves to combine humor, rhyme, and wordplay to create stories and songs that bring on the giggles.

You can find her books and animated sing-along song videos on her website for kids and kid-lovers—BiffBamBooza.com.

Biff Bam Booza books have received numerous awards and high acclaim, including Mom's Choice Gold, Purple Dragonfly, Eric Hoffer, and Literary Titan book awards, Readers' Favorite 5-star ratings, and Kirkus Review Magazine features.

Cheryl lives in Tucson, Arizona, and spends summers in her native New Jersey.

About the Illustrator

Nate Fakes sold his first drawing in the fifth grade for five dollars, sparking a lifelong passion for cartooning. His love for illustration, storytelling, and writing grew over the years, leading him to a career as a professional cartoonist.

While attending Wright State University, he worked as an editorial intern at MAD Magazine in New York City, later contributing comics to MAD for over a decade. His work has been featured in The New York Times, Scholastic, Parade Magazine, major greeting card companies, and numerous other publications. He has also collaborated with well-known brands such as 21st Century Fox, the NFL, NBA, MLB, Costco, and Brecks.

His career brought him to Los Angeles, where he worked as a full-time cartoonist for Red Bull advertisements. His syndicated comic panel, Break of Day, is published daily in over 80 newspapers through King Features.

Nate is also the author of A Fade of Light, published by West Margin Press. He is a proud member of the National Cartoonists Society and ASIFA Hollywood.

We hope you enjoyed this

Biff Bam Booza story.

Reviews mean the world to us.

We'd be so grateful if you'd take a moment to scan this QR code and leave us one.

bit.ly/WATICS2-Review

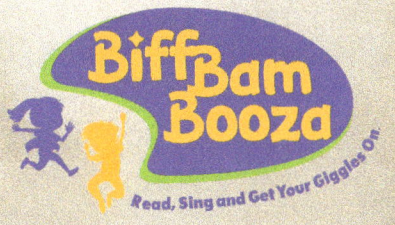

Copyright © 2025, Waterhole Productions LLC.
All rights reserved. No part of this publication may be reproduced, stored in a retrieval system, or transmitted in any form or by any means, electronic, mechanical, photocopying, recording or otherwise, without written permission of the copyright holder.

For more information regarding permission,
please write to BiffBamBooza@gmail.com.

Biff Bam Booza and associated logos
and trademarks are trademarks and/or
registered trademarks of Waterhole Productions LLC.

Publisher's Cataloging-in-Publication Data

Names: DaVeiga, Cheryl, author. | Fakes, Nate, illustrator.
Title: War at the ice cream store 2 : Rocky Road vs. The Sundae Storm / written by Cheryl DaVeiga; illustrated by Nate Fakes. Series: Biff Bam Booza
Description: Tucson, AZ: Waterhole Productions LLC, 2025. | Summary: The Ice Cream crew has to act quickly when there's an emergency at the ice cream shop.
Identifiers: LCCN: 2024922808 | ISBN: 978-1-958050-20-0 (hardcover) | 978-1-958050-19-4 (paperback) | 978-1-958050-18-7 (ebook)
Subjects: LCSH Ice cream--Juvenile fiction. | Emergencies--Juvenile fiction. | Humorous stories. | Graphic novels. | BISAC JUVENILE FICTION / Social Themes / Bullying | JUVENILE FICTION / Comics & Graphic Novels / Humorous | JUVENILE FICTION / Humorous Stories
Classification: LCC PZ7.1 .D38 Wa 2025 | DDC [E]--dc23